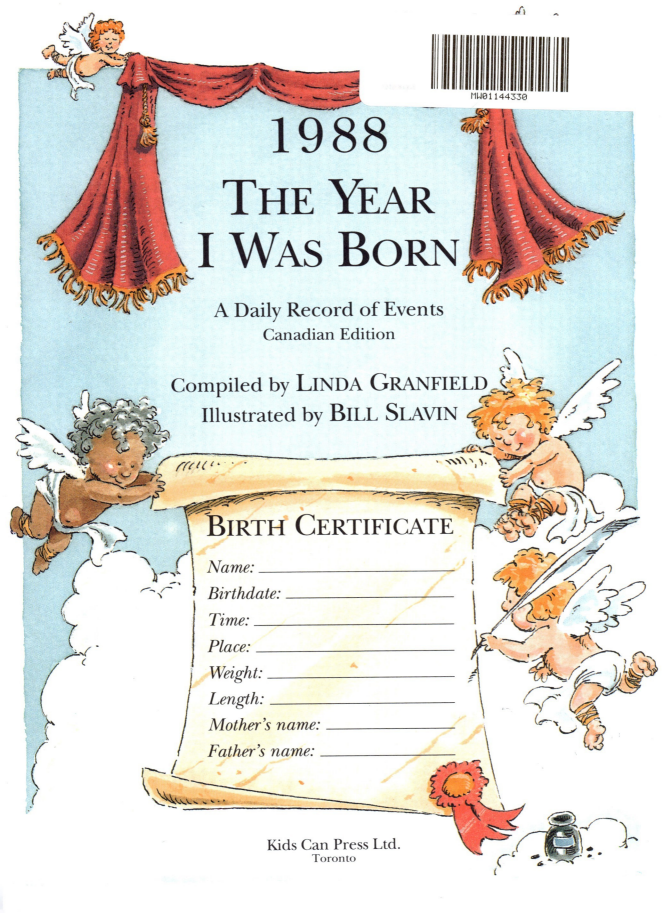

1988

THE YEAR
I WAS BORN

A Daily Record of Events
Canadian Edition

Compiled by LINDA GRANFIELD
Illustrated by BILL SLAVIN

BIRTH CERTIFICATE

Name: _____

Birthdate: _____

Time: _____

Place: _____

Weight: _____

Length: _____

Mother's name: _____

Father's name: _____

Kids Can Press Ltd.
Toronto

for Lori Burwash, with heartfelt gratitude for your wondrous forbearance and grace

---

The author wishes to thank the Social Sciences staff of the central branch of the Mississauga (Ontario) Public Library for their aid and co-operation in the research of this book.

Printed by permission of Signpost Books, Ltd., England

First Canadian edition published 1995

Canadian Cataloguing in Publication Data

Granfield, Linda
        1988, the year I was born : a daily record of events

Canadian ed.
ISBN 1-55074-192-6

1. Nineteen eighty-eight, A.D. - Chronology - Juvenile literature.
2. Canada - History - 1963-   - Chronology - Juvenile literature.*
I. Slavin, Bill.   II. Title.

FC630.G73   1995   j971.064'7   C95-930284-0
F1034.2.G73   1995

Kids Can Press Ltd.
29 Birch Avenue
Toronto, Ontario, Canada
M4V 1E2

Edited by Lori Burwash and Trudee Romanek
Designed by Esperança Melo
Printed and bound in Hong Kong

95 0 9 8 7 6 5 4 3 2 1

A Week of Birthdays

Monday's child is fair of face,
Tuesday's child is full of grace,
Wednesday's child is full of woe,
Thursday's child has far to go,
Friday's child is loving and giving,
Saturday's child works hard for its living,
But the child that's born on the Sabbath day
Is bonny and blithe, and good and gay.

The Days of the Week

Sunday — the sun's day

Monday — the moon's day

Tuesday — day of Tiu, or Tyr, the Norse god of war and the sky

Wednesday — Woden's day (Woden, or Odin, was the chief Norse god)

Thursday — Thor's day (in Norse mythology, Thor was the god of thunder)

Friday — Freya's day (Freya was a wife of Odin and the goddess of love and beauty)

Saturday — Saturn's day (in Roman mythology, Saturn was a harvest god)

The Months

January — the month of Janus, Roman god of doorways, who had two faces looking in opposite directions

February — the month of februa, a Roman festival of purification

March — the month of Mars, the Roman god of war

April — the month of Venus, the Roman goddess of love

May — the month of Maia, the Roman goddess of spring

June — the month of Juno, the principal Roman goddess

July — the month of Roman emperor Julius Caesar

August — the month of Roman emperor Augustus

September — the seventh (*septem*) month of the old Roman calendar

October — the eighth (*octo*) month of the old Roman calendar

November — the ninth (*novem*) month of the old Roman calendar

December — the tenth (*decem*) month of the old Roman calendar

Birthstones and Flowers

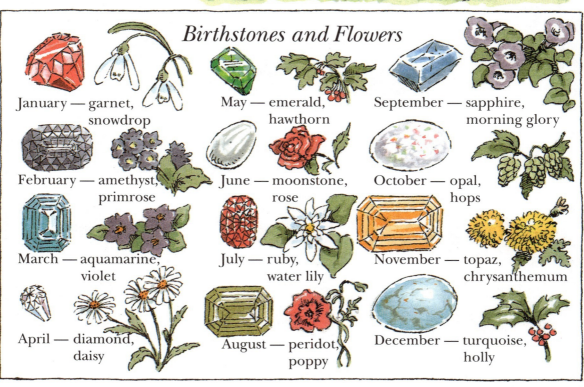

January — garnet, snowdrop

February — amethyst, primrose

March — aquamarine, violet

April — diamond, daisy

May — emerald, hawthorn

June — moonstone, rose

July — ruby, water lily

August — peridot, poppy

September — sapphire, morning glory

October — opal, hops

November — topaz, chrysanthemum

December — turquoise, holly

JANUARY

Extra! Extra!

World's Oldest Recipes???

Three clay slabs kept at Yale University are 4000 years old, and scientists believe that they're the oldest "cookbooks" in the world. Figures scratched into the Mesopotamian slabs give instructions for making rich foods, such as stew thickened with blood, and for preparing meats such as gazelle and a bird called tarru. Is that for here or to go?

Top Baby Names 1988

Boys	Girls
Michael	Amanda
Matthew	Jessica
Christopher	Sarah
Andrew	Ashley
David	Stephanie
Kyle	Jennifer
Daniel	Nicole
Ryan	Melissa
Justin	Samantha
Joshua	Laura

Trivia tidbit

Toronto's SkyDome will have the world's largest video-screen scoreboard, measuring 35 m by 10 m. That's three times bigger than the next largest, which is in Miami's Dolphin Stadium.

What's *that*?!? Haggis

A traditional Scottish dish served especially on Robbie Burns Night, haggis is a boiled pudding that looks like a big sausage. Oatmeal, liver, heart, onion and allspice are cooked in a sheep's stomach.

You said it!

"No comments from the peanut gallery."

In many theatres, long ago, only people in the cheapest seats at the back of the balcony could buy peanuts. Some people believed that only the opinions of the people sitting near the stage counted and that the people in the "peanut gallery" had less to contribute. The expression still refers to those whose advice or opinions some people think can be ignored.

JANUARY

Friday
1
New Year's Day
The Olympic torch is in Chatham, Ontario. There are 43 days to go until it reaches the Calgary Winter Olympics.

Saturday
2
Prime Minister Brian Mulroney and President Ronald Reagan sign a free-trade agreement between Canada and the United States. Parliament and Congress still have to approve the deal.
☆ **1932** — birth of Jean Little, author of *The Revenge of the Small Small*

Sunday
3
Poet Dennis Lee is writing lyrics for a new Muppets television series called "Fraggle Rock."
☆ **1939** — birth of Bobby Hull, hockey player

Monday
4
The Canadian junior hockey team wins gold in Moscow with a 3–2 victory over the Soviet squad.

Tuesday
5
For the first time in its 62-year history, New York's Radio City Rockettes' high-kicking chorus line will include a black dancer.

Wednesday
6
It's Sviat Vechir, or Christmas Eve, for Ukrainian-Canadian families. They traditionally serve a meatless meal of 12 dishes.

Thursday
7
There are no green eggs and ham, but there are plenty of pictures by Dr. Seuss. The Baltimore Museum is showing the artwork of Theodor Seuss Geisel and celebrating his 100 million books in print on Planet Earth.
☆ **1827** — birth of Sir Sandford Fleming, inventor, scientist, railway surveyor and engineer

Friday
8
"The pin man," Gary Wintraub, of Thornhill, Ontario, has 4000 minor-hockey pins in his collection and carries around in shopping bags another 2000 pins for trading.

Saturday
9
Canada's national women's volleyball team defeats the South Korean team 3–0 in the international invitational tournament in West Germany.
☆ **1802** — birth of Catharine Parr Traill, author of *The Backwoods of Canada*

Sunday
10
People are offering some of the 6000 Olympic torchbearers thousands of dollars to part with their red and white track suits and toques. So far, no sale.
☆ **1935** — birth of Ronnie Hawkins, singer-songwriter

Monday
11
The snowmaking plant at Mount Allan, Alberta, is working 24 hours a day to make the flakes that Mother Nature hasn't yet provided for the Olympic alpine skiing venue. Freeze-dried pellets, called Snomax, are mixed with water ... voilà, more snow.
☆ **1815** — birth of Sir John A. Macdonald, first prime minister of Canada
☆ **1934** — birth of Jean Chrétien, 20th prime minister of Canada

JANUARY

Tuesday 12
British mountain climbers announce a new expedition up Mount Everest to clean up the hundreds of empty oxygen and fuel cylinders left by other mountaineers.

Wednesday 13
"La Bamba," the song made famous by Ritchie Valens in the 1950s, is popular again. It has revived the colourful Latin look in fashion and the spicy flavours of Spanish foods.

Thursday 14
Kirstin Swanson, 12, takes the Olympic torch from Ontario into Manitoba by snowmobile for its three-day trek across the province.
☆ 1855 — birth of Homer Watson, painter

Friday 15
Justine Blainey, 15, debuts on defence with the Toronto East Enders after a two-year battle to win the right to play in the previously all-male hockey league.
☆ 1947 — birth of Veronica Tennant, ballet dancer

Saturday 16
The Royal Ontario Museum opens its new Bat Cave, a re-creation of a cave in Jamaica, complete with 3500 wax and vinyl bats and computer-controlled lights and action.
☆ 1948 — birth of Cliff Thorburn, champion snooker player

Sunday 17
Torchbearers carry the Olympic flame into Regina, 25 days before the Calgary Winter Olympics begin.
☆ 1958 — birth of Andrea Wayne–von Königslöw, author of *Frogs*

Monday 18
Prince Edward Islanders vote in favour of a bridge or tunnel to connect the island to the mainland.
☆ 1939 — birth of David French, playwright

Tuesday 19
Yellowknife welcomes the Olympic flame to the Northwest Territories with a special ceremony.
☆ 1934 — birth of Lloyd Robertson, T.V. anchor and reporter

Wednesday 20
The Olympic flame crosses into British Columbia from the Northwest Territories, but spends most of its first day in B.C. in a plane headed to Vancouver Island.
☆ 1946 — birth of Peter Eyvindson, author of *The Wish Wind*

Thursday 21
In Halifax, 65 student choir members are practising for their Olympic Youth Music Showcase performances. They're the only Nova Scotia school group invited to the Calgary Winter Olympics.
☆ 1937 — birth of Jim Unger, cartoonist and creator of "Herman"

JANUARY

Friday 22

The Soviet Union is launching Tetris, its first commercial computer game, in North America. Software specialists predict a major success.

☆ **1957** — birth of Mike Bossy, hockey player

Saturday 23

Special delivery for cosmonauts! An unattended cargo-transport rocket loaded with food, fuel — and mail — docks with the orbiting Soviet space station *Mir*.

☆ **1929** — birth of John Polanyi, professor and co-winner of a Nobel Prize for Chemistry

Sunday 24

The "man in motion," Rick Hansen, attaches the Olympic torch to his wheelchair and begins his trip from Vancouver to North Vancouver.

☆ **1942** — birth of Sandy Frances Duncan, author of *Listen to Me, Grace Kelly*

Monday 25

It's Robbie Burns Night, and thousands of Canadians celebrate their Scottish heritage by eating haggis and singing "Auld Lang Syne," Burns's most famous song.

Tuesday 26

A plan to take the sexism out of "O Canada" is defeated for the third time in the House of Commons. If passed, the line "in all our sons command" would have become "in all of us command."

☆ **1961** — birth of Wayne Gretzky, hockey player

Wednesday 27

The Canadian Olympic Association announces the names of the 117 Canadian athletes who will compete in the Calgary Winter Olympics. It's Canada's largest team ever.

☆ **1953** — birth of Frank Augustyn, ballet dancer

Thursday 28

Steve Fonyo, the cross-Canada runner who lost a leg to cancer, carries the Olympic torch in his home town of Vernon, British Columbia.

☆ **1822** — birth of Alexander Mackenzie, second prime minister of Canada

Friday 29

Toronto celebrates Frostfest '88, a weekend of pancake breakfasts, skating parties and ice-castle sculptures. Problems?? There's no snow, and the temperatures are so high they break a 72-year record!

Saturday 30

A new commemorative silver dollar honours Canada's first ironworks, Les Forges du Saint-Maurice, Quebec, which was built in 1738. The coin shows two blacksmiths striking iron on an anvil.

Sunday 31

It's Super Bowl Sunday. The Washington Redskins beat the Denver Broncos 42–10.

☆ **1928** — birth of Gathie Falk, multimedia artist

FEBRUARY

Extra! Extra!

Jamaica Sends Bobsled Team to Winter Olympics

People may chuckle at the idea of a bobsled team from a country that never sees snow, but the Jamaican team is serious about Olympic competition. The team started racing in push-cart derbies in Kingston, Jamaica, and has spent the last three months getting ready for the big event. It raised $25 000 for a bobsled and has arrived in Calgary for more practice — this time on snow!

Groundhog Day

In medieval Europe, February 2 was known as Candlemas Day, a festival named for the custom of lighting candles on that day.

People believed that the weather on Candlemas Day foretold the weather for the following weeks. Now, February 2 is called Groundhog Day, and North Americans rely on groundhogs to predict when spring will arrive — even though scientists say groundhogs are correct only 37 per cent of the time.

Trivia tidbit

An estimated 1.5 billion people, one-third of the world's population, watched the televised opening ceremonies of the 1988 Calgary Winter Olympics.

What's *that*?!?   Chinook

Chinook is a Native word meaning "snow eater," and when this wind blows east of the Rockies, it does just that — the warm, dry wind can eat up, or melt, lots of snow in minutes.

You said it!

"*Citius, Altius, Fortius*" The Latin words in this Olympic motto mean "faster, higher, braver," or, according to the more modern interpretation, "swifter, higher, stronger." Father Didon, a French educator, wrote the motto in 1895, the year before the first modern Olympic Games were held in Athens, Greece.

Monday 1

The Black Cultural Society of Nova Scotia is planning displays and a show of dance, music and rap to celebrate Black History Month.
☆ **1882** — birth of Louis St. Laurent, 12th prime minister of Canada

Tuesday 2

Groundhog Day
Ontario's Wiarton Willie makes it official. The groundhog didn't see his shadow under cloudy skies, so it's going to be an early spring.

Wednesday 3

Pizza has gone from plain to fancy. It's called gourmet, designer or yuppie pizza, and the toppings include goat cheese, pesto, sun-dried tomatoes, even lobster and caviar.
☆ **1843** — birth of Sir William Van Horne, railway official

FEBRUARY

Thursday 4
Excitement builds as the Olympic flame enters Alberta. There are only nine more days until the Winter Olympics begin in Calgary.

Friday 5
Andre the Giant defeats Hulk Hogan and is awarded the WWF championship belt. Hulk's fans are angry because their hero wasn't even pinned to the canvas!

Saturday 6
U.S. teen millionaire Larry Adler visits Ottawa for a trade show. He owns and operates three businesses (including lawn care) and has four lawyers, but he still calls himself "a regular kid."

Sunday 7
It's so cold in Alberta that the government is feeding barley to about 45 000 mallard ducks who can't find food under the snow and ice.
☆ 1945 — birth of Colette Whiten, sculptor

Monday 8
At the International Toilet Forum in Tokyo, you can see toilet seats attached to statues and a bath-tub with a stereo, built-in library facilities and touch-sensitive controls.

Tuesday 9
Constable Misti Anthony, the first Native Canadian female police officer in Toronto, is sworn in.
☆ 1894 — birth of Billy Bishop, ace fighter pilot in World War I

Wednesday 10
In Saint John, New Brunswick, Canadian Brett Campbell wins the world amateur chess championship after 12 gruelling games.
☆ 1955 — birth of Brenda Clark, illustrator of *Little Fingerling*

Thursday 11
Governor General's Literary Awards go to illustrators Kim LaFave (*Amos's Sweater*) and Philippe Béha (*Les Jeux de Pic-Mots*) and writers Welwyn Wilton Katz (*The Third Magic*) and Michele Marineau (*Cassiopée ou l'Été*).

Friday 12
At last! The Olympic torch has travelled more than 18 000 km across Canada and will light the BIG flame in Calgary tomorrow.
☆ 1959 — birth of Bill Slavin, the illustrator of this book

Saturday 13
The 15th Winter Olympics open in Calgary. As Native musicians beat drums, 12-year-old Robyn Percy, of Calgary, lights the cauldron with the Olympic flame.
☆ 1925 — birth of Gerald Tailfeathers, one of the first Native Canadians to become a professional artist

Sunday 14
Valentine's Day
Meryl Dinsmore, of Toronto, gets her 61st mystery valentine since 1928. The postmark is from Sweden, and the card is signed "Your Secret Admirer."
☆ 1931 — birth of Dorothy Joan Harris, author of *No Dinosaurs in the Park*

Monday 15
It's Multicultural and Heritage Week! In British Columbia, people kick off the week with Native dancing, ethnic foods, cultural seminars and traditional costumes from around the world.

Tuesday 16
Statistics Canada reports that Canadians are skiing more than ever. Thirty-five per cent of Canadian households own skis and are spending more time on the slopes in winter.

FEBRUARY

Wednesday 17
Chinese New Year
Wayne Gretzky ties Gordie Howe's all-time mark of 1049 career assists.
☆ **1820** — birth of Elzéar-Alexandre Taschereau, first Canadian cardinal

Thursday 18
The National Film Board's animated short films *George and Rosemary* and *L'homme Qui Plantait des Arbres/The Man Who Planted Trees* have been nominated for an Academy Award.
☆ **1916** — birth of Jean Drapeau, mayor of Montreal during the 1967 World Expo and the 1976 Summer Olympics

Friday 19
Karen Percy, of Banff, Alberta, wins the Olympic bronze medal in women's downhill skiing. She missed winning silver by one-hundredth of a second!

Saturday 20
Brian Orser, of Penetanguishene, Ontario, wins the Olympic silver medal in men's figure skating.
☆ **1887** — birth of Vincent Massey, 18th governor general of Canada

Sunday 21
More than 400 workers clean up over 180 t of trash each day in Calgary during the Olympics. They collect it in special acrylic bags that won't split in the cold.

Monday 22
Karen Percy wins her second bronze medal, in the women's super slalom. That's two medals in her first Olympics.
☆ **1948** — birth of Paul Kropp, author of *Ellen/Elena/Luna*

Tuesday 23
Tracy Wilson, of Port Moody, British Columbia, and her partner Rob McCall, of Dartmouth, Nova Scotia, win the Olympic bronze medal in ice dancing.
☆ **1949** — birth of Marc Garneau, Canada's first astronaut

Wednesday 24
Toad A, who lives in an Iowa zoo, has been recognized as the world's largest toad. The 2.3-kg toad will appear in the next *Guinness Book of World Records*.
☆ **1866** — birth of Martha Black, Yukon naturalist and the second woman elected to Parliament

Thursday 25
Listed for sale in Canadian newspapers: a 30-room castle in Belgium. Built mid-1800s, 18 bedrooms, 10 bathrooms, 2 elevators and a forest. Only $3.5 million.

Friday 26
Great news! China announces that new bamboo has started to grow in the endangered pandas' three native provinces.
☆ **1961** — birth of Vicki Keith, marathon swimmer

Saturday 27
Elizabeth Manley, of Gloucester, Ontario, wins an Olympic silver medal in women's figure skating.
☆ **1899** — birth of Charles Best, co-discoverer of insulin

Sunday 28
K.d. lang sings a square-dance tune at the closing ceremonies of the Calgary Winter Olympics, and the Olympic flame is extinguished.
☆ **1712** — birth of Louis-Joseph de Montcalm, French military leader

Monday 29
Leap Year Day
She scores! The first episode of Carol Bolt's radio play, *Icetime*, airs. It's about 15-year-old Justine Blainey's two-year struggle to play on a boys hockey team.

Extra! Extra!

Orchestra Pours Tunes from Tumblers

The four members of Toronto's Glass Orchestra make music from an assortment of glass goblets, beakers, test tubes, bowls and dishes. Since the musicians' instruments can break easily, the tunes they play depend on what isn't broken. They are the only glass musicians in the world who write and perform their own music, but making music from glass objects dates back at least 2000 years. The musicians wet their fingers and rub, tap or ping the glass pieces. "We're the terrors of a china shop," chuckles one musician.

Top *T.V. Programs 1988*

- "The Cosby Show"
- "Roseanne"
- "A Different World"
- "Cheers"
- "60 Minutes"
- "The Golden Girls"
- "Who's the Boss?"
- "Murder, She Wrote"
- "Empty Nest"
- "Anything but Love"

Trivia tidbit

Metropolitan Toronto's 1988 telephone book is the biggest ever: more than 2000 pages with more than 1 million numbers. It used 6400 t of paper, 38.4 t of glue and 99.7 t of ink.

What's *that*?!?   Daedalus

In a Greek myth, Daedalus and his son, Icarus, escaped from prison by building wings for themselves. Despite Daedalus' warning, Icarus flew too close to the sun, the wax in his wings melted, and he fell into the sea. Daedalus got safely to an island.

You said it!

"You're barking up the wrong tree." Hunting dogs sometimes mislead hunters by barking at the bottom of a tree that they mistakenly think has an animal in its branches. If someone tells you that you're barking up the wrong tree, it means you're following a false lead or clue.

MARCH

Tuesday 1
Wayne Gretzky celebrates in Edmonton after breaking Gordie Howe's NHL record of career assists. The Great One has 1050 assists in only nine seasons.
☆ **1947** — birth of Alan Thicke, actor

Wednesday 2
Quarterama, Canada's biggest Quarter Horse show, opens in Toronto. Nearly 4000 horses compete.
☆ **1948** — birth of Camilla Gryski, author of *Friendship Bracelets*

Thursday 3
Purim
A Canadian-Soviet scientific team begins a 2000-km ski trek, dubbed "Polar Bridge," across the top of the world.
☆ **1847** — birth of Alexander Graham Bell, inventor of the telephone

Friday 4
It's World Day of Prayer, and people of all major denominations in 170 countries and regions gather to pray for peace and justice.
☆ **1901** — birth of Wilbur Franks, inventor of the "G suit," which was later refined for astronauts

Saturday 5
Fifty-two dog teams start the 1760-km Iditarod Trail Sled Dog Race from Anchorage to Nome, Alaska.

Sunday 6
A peacock community has roosted in a Victoria, British Columbia, subdivision. The peacocks are so comfortable they're sleeping outside with housecats, but residents aren't too sure about the mess and noise the birds make.
☆ **1940** — birth of Ken Danby, artist

Monday 7
Toronto Blue Jays fans as young as 11 years old audition for jobs as seventh-inning stretchers. The 12 finalists will work for about two minutes during each of the 40 regular-season games.

Tuesday 8
International Women's Day
It's always Hockey Night in Michael Birtheimer's home in Hamilton, Ontario. The fan has built a miniature hockey arena — complete with 12 000 spectators — in his dining room!

Wednesday 9
Hot albums and cassettes include those by Tiffany, John Cougar Mellencamp, Sting and Michael Jackson.

Thursday 10
The Polar Bridge group has completed 90 km of its trip across the top of the world despite broken skis, -47°C temperatures and clothes that just won't dry inside igloos.
☆ **1947** — birth of Kim Campbell, 19th (and first woman) prime minister of Canada

Friday 11
In Ottawa, Olympic silver medalist Elizabeth Manley is honoured as athlete of the month for February. An arena near Ottawa has been named for her.
☆ **1943** — birth of Sharon Siamon, author of *Gallop for Gold*

MARCH

Saturday 12
For the second year in a row, Pierre Harvey of Quebec wins the 30-km cross-country ski race at the Swedish nordic ski games in Falun, Sweden.
☆ **1821** — birth of Sir John Abbott, third prime minister of Canada

Sunday 13
Donald Amyotte, 8, and his sister Renée, 10, of Edmonton, have each claimed $500 from their parents for going without television for a year.
☆ **1914** — birth of W.O. Mitchell, author of *Who Has Seen the Wind*

Monday 14
They're purple and shapeless, and they're popular T.V. personalities. The California Raisins, animated plastic figures, have captured North America's imagination. The shrivelled grapes even have a bestselling album!
☆ **1932** — birth of Norval Morrisseau, artist of Ojibwa ancestry

Tuesday 15
The Daily News, Montreal's new English tabloid newspaper, rolls its first 80 000 copies off the presses.
☆ **1943** — birth of David Cronenberg, film maker

Wednesday 16
Susan Butcher wins the Iditarod Trail Sled Dog Race for the third time in a row.
The Alaskan took 11 days, 11 hours, 41 minutes — and won more than $30 000.
☆ **1934** — birth of Ramon Hnatyshyn, 24th governor general of Canada

Thursday 17
St. Patrick's Day
Explorers George Vancouver and Simon Fraser are featured on new stamps released today to celebrate the exploration of Canada.

Friday 18
Movie fans are enjoying the popular hits *Vice-Versa, Johnny Be Good, Wall Street* and *Moonstruck.*
☆ **1869** — birth of Maude Abbott, an acclaimed pathologist barred from medicine because she was a woman

Saturday 19
The great Olympic garage sale in Calgary continues. For sale: used Olympic goods such as phones, boots, clothing with the Olympic insignia, and larger items, such as computers.

Sunday 20
Spring Equinox
"Edible landscaping" is catching on. People are planning gardens that can be both looked at and eaten. How about some Purple Ruffle Basil or Little Sweetheart Strawberries?
☆ **1939** — birth of Brian Mulroney, 18th prime minister of Canada

Monday 21
Movie and T.V. fans in Toronto keep their eyes open! Leonard Nimoy, Diane Keaton, Al Pacino and Christopher Plummer are in town filming projects.

MARCH

Tuesday
22

Horoscopes for dogs are available in Paris for the first time. The Astrodog division of the Society for the Thinking Dog will do a ten-page zodiacal analysis of your pet, for a fee.
☆ **1909** — birth of Gabrielle Roy, author of *The Tin Flute*

Wednesday
23

Buffalo meat, once the major source of meat for the Plains Indians and early settlers, is now considered "health food." In Winnipeg, it can be delivered right to your door.
☆ **1951** — birth of Peter Cumming, author of *A Horse Called Farmer*

Thursday
24

Two men from the London Zoo, in England, set off for the island of Saint Helena to search for the world's largest earwig. The 7.6-cm insect hasn't been seen for 20 years, and nobody knows if it is still living!
☆ **1936** — birth of David Suzuki, geneticist and broadcaster

Friday
25

Kurt Browning, from Caroline, Alberta, completes the first-ever quadruple jump (a toe loop with four revolutions in the air, landing on one blade) done in competition, at the world figure skating championships in Budapest, Hungary.
☆ **1966** — birth of Jeff Healey, singer-songwriter

Saturday
26

Members of the Australian Dalmatian Club, wearing T-shirts to match their pets' spots, celebrate the relaunch of the Walt Disney animated film *One Hundred and One Dalmatians*.
☆ **1951** — birth of Martin Short, actor and comedian

Sunday
27

Canada's Greek communities celebrate the 167th anniversary of Greek independence with parades and other local festivities.

Monday
28

Twenty-three wood bison have been released into the Yukon wild in an effort to create a free, roaming herd similar to those found in other parts of western Canada.
☆ **1951** — birth of Karen Kain, dancer

Tuesday
29

Rick Hansen, Canada's "man in motion" who raised funds for spinal cord research, receives the Order of Canada from Governor General Jeanne Sauvé in Ottawa.
☆ **1945** — birth of Margaret Buffie, author of *My Mother's Ghost*

Wednesday
30

Marketing researchers report that by the year 2001, automobiles will have microwave compartments instead of glove compartments — so drivers can eat a hot breakfast on the way to work.

Thursday
31

The *Daedalus*, a human-powered aircraft, makes a successful test run in Crete. The pilot hopes to fly from Crete to Santorini, a record distance of 119 km.
☆ **1950** — birth of Ian Wallace, illustrator of *The Year of Fire*

APRIL

Extra! Extra!

Now *That's* a Big Family!

Susie Smith spent 100 of her 105 years in North Preston, Nova Scotia, and at her recent passing, newspapers recorded the remarkable legacy she left behind. Susie raised 19 children and is survived by 1 son, 4 daughters, 84 grandchildren, 350 great-grandchildren, 250 great-great-grandchildren and 10 great-great-great-grandchildren. That's a lot of hugs to share!

Academy Awards Winners

Millions of viewers around the world watched the film industry celebrate Oscar Night, the evening of the Academy Awards. The major awards were:
☆ Best Actor — Michael Douglas, in *Wall Street*
☆ Best Actress — Cher, in *Moonstruck*
☆ Best Picture — *The Last Emperor*

Trivia tidbit
In 1988, half a million children watched "Mr. Dressup" (Ernie Coombs) on T.V. every day.

What's *that*?!? Yuppie
Baby boomers (people born in the 1950s and 1960s) were given this name in the 1980s, when they earned and spent a lot of money. *Yuppie* is an acronym for "**y**oung **u**rban **p**rofessional."

You said it!
"How about a baker's dozen?"

Doughnuts are often advertised as "a baker's dozen," or 13 doughnuts, rather than 12, for a set price. The extra doughnut comes from the days when bakers paid fines for shortchanging customers — in case their flour was lightweight, bakers tossed in an extra bun.

Friday
1
April Fool's Day
Thousands gather on the streets of Toronto's Italian community for one of North America's largest Good Friday processions.

Saturday
2
Passover begins
Daylight savings time starts, and clock hands are moved ahead one hour. Across Canada, people remind themselves "spring ahead, fall back."

Sunday
3
Easter
Sugarless gum is 25 years old! Tony Bilotti invented Trident after nine years, 6500 hours of research, 360 trial batches and 22 680 kg of gum. (He sold the formula in 1963 for $1, a common practice at the time.)

APRIL

Monday 4
The Toronto Blue Jays and the Kansas City Royals open the American League baseball season in Kansas City. (The Jays win 5–3.)
☆ **1940** — birth of Phoebe Gilman, author of *Jillian Jiggs*

Tuesday 5
Alert! World Wildlife Fund announces that pandas are closer to extinction, even with the bamboo that has begun to grow in their native provinces.

Wednesday 6
What a day for news! Instant noodles are 30 years old, tiramisu (an Italian treat with ladyfingers, coffee and creamy cheese) is the trendy dessert, and *Beetlejuice* is the top movie.

Thursday 7
Figure skater Elizabeth Manley says her childhood dream is coming true: she's about to begin a professional skating career with the Ice Capades.
☆ **1851** — birth of John Bengough, political cartoonist

Friday 8
The Polar Bridge team continues its trek across the top of the world and is now 340 km from the North Pole.

Saturday 9
Kids in Kings Landing, New Brunswick, are learning at the local living-history museum what life was like 150 years ago. The costumed students help milk cows, spin wool and churn butter.

Sunday 10
Canadian Ian Millar and Big Ben, his 12-year-old Belgian gelding, win the World Cup show-jumping final at Goteborg, Sweden.

Monday 11
It's Academy Awards night in Los Angeles. The National Film Board's *L'homme Qui Plantait des Arbres/The Man Who Planted Trees* wins the Best Animated Short Film award.
☆ **1914** — birth of Norman McLaren, director of animated films

Tuesday 12
Vaisakhi, the Sikh New Year, begins, and the Canadian Sikh community celebrates with prayer services. In Toronto, Sikhs collect supplies for food banks and plan a parade.

Wednesday 13
Canadians are the third largest mushroom eaters in the world. Each Canadian eats 3.1 kg of sliced, diced, raw or cooked mushrooms a year.

Thursday 14
It's Aggie (Agricultural) Day in Calgary, and some city kids are getting a chance to pull wool, cuddle chicks, taste homemade yogurt, and even see a horse for the first time at Stampede Park's Agriculture Pavilion.

Friday 15
Cody Green, 12, has Flames fever! The Calgary Flames are in the Stanley Cup playoffs, so Cody's sporting a brush cut with the "flaming C" shaved into it.

Saturday 16
Prom dresses fill department stores ... but not for long. Bestsellers include bubble and strapless styles, iridescent colours and big bustle bows.
☆ **1907** — birth of J. Armand Bombardier, inventor of the snowmobile

Sunday 17
Vancouver's Kyle Brady, 12, wins the grand prize in the *Vancouver Sun Run* — a new car! But until he has a licence, his family will drive him around.
☆ **1943** — birth of Bobby Curtola, Canada's first teen singing idol

APRIL

Monday 18
Disco and breakdancing are all the rage in Beijing. Some Chinese teens have seen the movie *Breakdance* more than eight times!
☆ 1953 — birth of Rick Moranis, actor

Tuesday 19
The Handlebar (moustache) Club in England meets for its annual dinner. Members must have "a hirsute appendage with graspable extremities."
☆ 1953 — birth of Patricia Quinlan, author of *Tiger Flowers*

Wednesday 20
Queen Elizabeth has received 110 maple trees from the Canadian government. They'll be planted at two of her homes, Windsor and Balmoral castles.
☆ 1949 — birth of Toller Cranston, figure skater and artist

Thursday 21
Israel celebrates its 40th Independence Day and receives tributes from Canada's House of Commons.
☆ 1964 — birth of Alex Baumann, champion swimmer

Friday 22
Earth Day
A new French perfume for babies is the latest yuppie fad. Ptisenbon (phonetic French for "baby smells nice") costs $30 for 93 g.
☆ 1952 — birth of Kathy Stinson, author of *The Bare Naked Book*

Saturday 23
In New York City, an auction of pop artist Andy Warhol's collection begins. Want to buy 316 watches or 114 cookie jars or a Superman touch-tone phone?
☆ 1897 — birth of Lester Pearson, 14th prime minister of Canada

Sunday 24
Holy cow! A trucker helps Ontario police round up cattle escapees. When the cattle start to graze beside a road, police head them off.

Monday 25
Plans are under way in Parrsboro, Nova Scotia, to build a museum for local dinosaur fossils that rival the fossils found in the Alberta Badlands.

Tuesday 26
The Polar Bridge ski team reaches the North Pole and raises the Soviet and Canadian flags. Before continuing its trek across the top of the world, the team feasts on vacuum-packed coq au vin and pâté.
☆ 1922 — birth of Jeanne Sauvé, 23rd (and first woman) governor general of Canada

Wednesday 27
Fashion-conscious kids are wearing longer shorts, called jams, to school.
☆ 1954 — birth of Jan Hudson, author of *Dawn Rider*

Thursday 28
While building a clubhouse, eight Dutch children dig up jars filled with gold coins and jewellery worth more than $250 000. If the owners aren't found within 30 years, the kids can keep the loot.
☆ 1935 — birth of Robert "Bob" White, labour leader

Friday 29
It's Arbour Day, and schoolchildren in Toronto spend part of their day planting trees to celebrate.

Saturday 30
Six hundred million people around the world watch as Quebec chanteuse Céline Dion, 20, wins the Eurovision Song Contest in Dublin, Ireland — by one point!
☆ 1947 — birth of Kit Pearson, author of *Looking at the Moon*

MAY

Extra! Extra!

Around the World in 80 Minutes

A group of Canadian and American athletes was transported to the top of the world to run around the North Pole. The run, organized by 62-year-old "Arctic Joe" Womersley, of Toronto, was planned to coincide with the recent Soviet-Canadian Polar Bridge expedition across the top of the world. Despite cold temperatures and hip-deep snow, the runners completed their 10-km course in only 80 minutes. Some have pieces of the North Pole in their freezers to prove it!

May Day

For about three thousand years, the first of May has traditionally been the day to celebrate the new season. People often erect ribbon-decorated maypoles, which symbolize trees, and dance around them. In some countries, May Day is a holiday. In France, lovers exchange flowers on May 1. And at dawn on May Day in Toronto's High Park, dancers, musicians and lots of onlookers greet the day with plenty of merriment.

Trivia tidbit

The Osborne Collection of early children's books, in Toronto, has more than 16 000 books, including a 160-year-old schoolbook and a copy of *Aesop's Fables* from the 1300s.

What's *that*?!? Wampum

North American Native people made beads from polished white shells and called them *wampum*. They were used for jewellery and money, and were strung in special patterns to record events and agreements.

You said it!

"Everything was above-board."

This expression comes from the days when gamblers used card tricks to win money. If their hands were below the table (or board), they could cheat, but if their hands were "above-board," everyone could see that they played an honest game. If something is above-board, it's honest and fair.

MAY

Sunday 1
Canadian teen Helen Kelesi wins the Citta di Taranto clay court women's tennis tournament.
☆ **1831** — birth of Emily Stowe, the first Canadian woman to practise medicine in Canada

Monday 2
Eight Micronesian men arrive in Japan after paddling the Pacific Ocean for 5280 km in a wooden canoe without any modern navigational aids.
☆ **1927** — birth of Budge Wilson, author of *The Leaving*

Tuesday 3
Pop artist Andy Warhol's collection, including 114 cookie jars, has been sold for more than $25 million. That's a lot of cookies!
☆ **1913** — birth of Joyce Barkhouse, author of *Pit Pony*

Wednesday 4
Dominion Sports Marketing of Calgary is *still* filling orders for commemorative pins ordered during the Winter Olympics ... and the Seoul Summer Olympics pins are about to arrive!
☆ **1929** — birth of Eric Wright, mystery writer

Thursday 5
In the "Archie" comic strip, famous shopper Veronica Lodge visits West Edmonton Mall, the world's largest shopping centre, with her father. "Daddy! You do know my weakness!" gasps Veronica.
☆ **1843** — birth of William Beers, a dentist who campaigned to have lacrosse accepted as Canada's national game

Friday 6
World Wildlife Fund offers an acre of Costa Rican rain forest, and everything in it, for $25 as an unusual and environmental Mother's Day gift.

Saturday 7
Summer movie releases are announced: *Big Top Pee-Wee*, *Funny Farm* and *Who Framed Roger Rabbit*.

Sunday 8
Eleven wampum belts are returned to the Six Nations Iroquois Confederacy in Ohsweken, Ontario, 90 years after they disappeared. The belts recorded agreements made between the Native people, the British and the French. They were found in an American museum.

Monday 9
Quack! Quack! People are still finding some of the 16 000 rubber ducks dropped last weekend into Ontario's Thames River to raise funds for heart and stroke research.
☆ **1928** — birth of Barbara Ann Scott, Olympic figure skater

Tuesday 10
Quebec's musical impersonator André-Philippe Gagnon wows a Vancouver audience with some of his 300 sounds and voices, including his one-man 18-voice rendition of "We Are the World."
☆ **1958** — birth of Gaëtan Boucher, Olympic speed skater

MAY

Wednesday
11
Irving Berlin celebrates his 100th birthday. The composer has published 1500 songs (only half of what he's written!), including such popular tunes as "White Christmas" and "Easter Parade."
☆ **1943** — birth of Nancy Greene, Olympic alpine skier

Thursday
12
Staff members of the Metropolitan Toronto Zoo say they're ready to deliver the more than 1000 "zoo babies" expected to arrive — almost hourly — during the spring baby boom. Already there are six newborn wood bison.
☆ **1921** — birth of Farley Mowat, author of *Curse of the Viking Grave*

Friday
13
Wedding bells ring on "Sesame Street" as characters Maria and Luis tie the knot!
☆ **1904** — birth of Earle Birney, poet

Saturday
14
In France, Canadian officials explore the *Amethyste,* the world's smallest nuclear-powered submarine. It's 73 m long and only 7.5 m wide and has a crew of 70 people.

Sunday
15
Just north of Toronto, the East Indian community unveils a 2.4-m statue of Indian leader Mahatma Gandhi in a parkette dedicated to peace and non-violence.

Monday
16
The Milk International Children's Festival, a week of colourful theatre, original music and creative dance for kids, opens in Toronto.

Tuesday
17
Twenty galleries and museums across Canada celebrate Group of Seven artist A.J. Casson's 90th birthday with special tributes.
☆ **1898** — birth of A.J. Casson, painter and member of the Group of Seven

Wednesday
18
Newfoundland teen Richard Lush is ahead after the first round of the Canadian National Monopoly championships in Toronto.
☆ **1957** — birth of Sharon Wood, the first woman from the Western Hemisphere to climb Mount Everest

Thursday
19
Cara Buffett, 9, of North Sydney, Nova Scotia, is the youngest player ever to compete in the Canadian National Monopoly championships. She defeats ten rivals and wins the title.
☆ **1952** — birth of Sarah Ellis, author of *The Baby Project*

Friday
20
On Parliament Hill, Prime Minister Brian Mulroney signs autographs and launches Fitweek, an awareness program run by Fitness Canada.
☆ **1940** — birth of Stan Mikita, hockey player

Saturday
21
The ceremonial ribbon is snipped, and the new National Gallery of Canada opens in Ottawa.
☆ **1928** — birth of Adele Wiseman, author

MAY

Sunday 22
In Montreal, Arlene Antoine becomes the first black woman to graduate from the Quebec Police Academy.

Monday 23
Victoria Day
Barbara Rusch, of Toronto, celebrates Queen Victoria's birthday in style — by wearing a bracelet made of hair which was given to Victoria in 1874 by Princess Beatrice, the ruler's daughter. (Barbara bought the bracelet at an auction for more than $2100.)

Tuesday 24
Talk about a big baby! A three-day-old giraffe born at Audubon Zoo, in New Orleans, is already 2 m tall and weighs 70 kg.
☆ 1930 — birth of Robert Bateman, painter

Wednesday 25
Need homework help? Ravi Vakil, 18, of Etobicoke, Ontario, has defeated 389 012 high-school math whizzes to become the first Canadian to win the American Mathematical Olympiad.
☆ 1879 — birth of Max Aitken (Lord Beaverbrook), politician and publisher

Thursday 26
The Edmonton Oilers defeat the Boston Bruins and win the Stanley Cup for the fourth time in five years.
☆ 1938 — birth of Teresa Stratas, opera singer

Friday 27
Vancouver's buzzing with movie stars filming five feature films — John Travolta, Kirstie Alley, John Candy, Corey Haim and Ted Danson are in town.
☆ 1945 — birth of Bruce Cockburn, singer-songwriter

Saturday 28
The Winnipeg International Children's Festival, featuring crafts and entertainers, continues in Kildonan Park.
☆ 1947 — birth of Lynn Johnston, cartoonist and creator of "For Better or For Worse"

Sunday 29
In Montreal, teen athlete Allison Higson, of Ontario, sets a new world record in the women's 200-m breaststroke at the Esso Cup Olympic trials.

Monday 30
Mother Teresa visits Vancouver to set up a mission for young mothers and an AIDS hospice.

Tuesday 31
After 89 days of travelling, the Polar Bridge team is only two days away from completing its trip across the top of the world.
☆ 1961 — birth of Corey Hart, singer-songwriter

JUNE

Extra! Extra!

How We Spend Our Time

People are amazed by — and are chuckling about — a recent U.S. study that gives some surprising statistics. It claims we spend five years of our lives waiting in line, six months sitting at traffic lights, one year looking for lost items, six years eating, eight months opening junk mail, four years doing housework, and two years trying to return phone calls!

The Hockey Hall of Fame

Each year, hockey players are selected by a special committee to join the Hockey Hall of Fame. In 1988, the four new members were Tony Esposito (Chicago Black Hawks), Guy Lafleur (Montreal Canadiens), Buddy O'Connor (Montreal Canadiens) and Brad Park (New York Rangers).

Trivia tidbit

In 1988, 300 000 readers in Canada, the United States, France, Italy and Britain enjoyed Canada's *Owl* magazine. What a hoot!

What's *that*?!?   Croquet

Croquet is an outdoor game played on grass or an official regulation lawn. Players use long-handled mallets to drive wooden balls through wickets.

You said it!

"You're like a bull in a china shop."

Some people say this expression, which is nearly two hundred years old, began with a fable about a donkey that broke a potter's goods. Others argue that it started with a political cartoon. Either way, things are usually left a mess! If you're like a bull in a china shop, you're clumsy.

JUNE

Wednesday
1
New stamps commemorating wildlife conservation and the 100th anniversary of Grey Owl's birth are released.

Thursday
2
Firecrackers and warm hugs mark the end of the Soviet-Canadian trek over the North Pole. The group is the first to make the trans-Arctic trip without vehicles or sled dogs. It took 91 days.

Friday
3
Pass the crayons! Metropolitan Toronto schoolchildren are busy making 6000 cards welcoming media and other visitors to the upcoming Economic Summit.
☆ **1954** — birth of Dan Hill, singer-songwriter

Saturday
4
Bill Phillips, the first Canadian to play major-league baseball (in 1879), is honoured with membership in the Canadian Baseball Hall of Fame.
☆ **1948** — birth of Sandra Post, professional golfer

Sunday
5
The Russian Orthodox Church celebrates 1000 years of Russian faith with a service opening the millennium.
☆ **1939** — birth of Joe Clark, 16th prime minister of Canada

Monday
6
Barbara Smucker, author of *Underground to Canada,* wins the Vicky Metcalf Award for her body of work in children's literature.
☆ **1935** — birth of Joy Kogawa, author of *Naomi's Road*

Tuesday
7
The Canadian pop trio Butterfly wins an award for best disco music at the Tokyo Music Festival for the song "What Kind of Fool."
☆ **1929** — birth of John Turner, 17th prime minister of Canada

Wednesday
8
Mario Lemieux of the Pittsburgh Penguins wins the Hart Trophy, ending fellow Canadian Wayne Gretzky's eight-year reign as the NHL's most valuable player.
☆ **1926** — birth of Queen Elizabeth II

Thursday
9
Prince Edward wears running shoes and overalls while he tours a Newfoundland hydroponic cucumber plant.

Friday
10
Everything's ready for the Formula I World Championship, the Grand Prix of Canada auto race in Montreal.
☆ **1637** — birth of Father Jacques Marquette, co-discoverer of the Mississippi River

JUNE

Saturday 11
Entertainers honour jailed South African leader Nelson Mandela in a ten-hour rock concert beamed from London to more than 51 countries.

Sunday 12
Almost 20 000 people gather in Metropolis, Illinois, to celebrate the 50th birthday of its home-town boy, Superman.
☆ **1921** — birth of James Houston, author-illustrator of *Long Claws*

Monday 13
Pioneer 10 marks its fifth anniversary as the first human-made spacecraft to leave the solar system.
☆ **1924** — birth of Harold Town, artist

Tuesday 14
In British Columbia, salmon-hatchery employees are extra busy with a bonanza number of returning salmon in the Capilano River. There are already five times the number of fish expected!
☆ **1924** — birth of Arthur Erickson, award-winning architect

Wednesday 15
In Montreal, the International Opera Festival makes plans to stage the opera *Aida* in Olympic Stadium on the largest theatrical stage ever built in North America. Five elephants and more than 1000 costumed performers will be on-stage.
☆ **1789** — birth of Josiah Henson, founder of an Ontario community for fugitive slaves

Thursday 16
The owner of a New Zealand china shop lets Colonel, an 1100-kg Hereford bull, roam about the store. Despite some hair-raising moments, none of the china is broken!
☆ **1874** — birth of Arthur Meighen, ninth prime minister of Canada

Friday 17
The new National Aviation Museum, featuring 107 aircraft representing Canadian and world aviation history, opens in Ottawa.

Saturday 18
Croquet Canada opens its new national headquarters at Hinder Estates in North York, Ontario.
☆ **1966** — birth of Kurt Browning, figure skating champion

Sunday 19
The three-day Economic Summit opens in Toronto. Canada hosts seven world leaders as they discuss agriculture, terrorism and drug issues.
☆ **1902** — birth of Guy Lombardo, musician and conductor

Monday 20
Summer Solstice
In Vancouver, Loretta the lobster is looking for a home. The 9.5-kg crustacean, thought to be 150 years old, arrived in a market's shipment from Prince Edward Island, but no one wants to eat her!
☆ **1945** — birth of Anne Murray, singer

JUNE

Tuesday 21
A pair of Dorothy's ruby slippers, from the movie *The Wizard of Oz*, sells for $165 000 at a New York auction, setting a world-record price for a movie prop.

Wednesday 22
The *hottest* summer movie, *Who Framed Roger Rabbit*, opens in air-conditioned theatres throughout Canada. The Walt Disney film combines live and animated action.

Thursday 23
Four teens from Quebec, British Columbia and Ontario have been chosen for the 1988 Canadian Chemistry Olympiad team. They'll take part in international competitions in Finland this summer.
☆ **1909** — birth of David Lewis, former leader of the New Democratic Party and one of Parliament's most powerful debaters

Friday 24
La Fête Nationale
More than 1000 Tremblays from across Canada, the United States and France begin a three-day family reunion in Chicoutimi, Quebec.
☆ **1963** — birth of Barbara Underhill, Olympic figure skater

Saturday 25
Twenty-year-old Quebec singer Céline Dion celebrates her English singing debut in Toronto. Dion, from a musical family of 14 people, started her career when she was 12 years old.
☆ **1945** — birth of Robert Charlebois, singer-songwriter

Sunday 26
Cory Porhownik loves his job. The government pays the Lockport, Manitoba, teen to take daily samples from the Red River, which is near his home, and to check them for temperature and quality. To get samples, he pulls himself in a cable car — hanging 12 m over the water — to the centre of the river. Yikes!
☆ **1854** — birth of Sir Robert Borden, eighth prime minister of Canada

Monday 27
Want to buy a museum? Albertan Belmore H. Schultz, 97, is selling his. The museum includes a World War II bomber, an emu egg, coins, a stuffed two-headed calf and about 50 000 other items.

Tuesday 28
Sarah Ferguson, the Duchess of York, is writing two children's books about a helicopter named Budgie.

Wednesday 29
Would you like to play with items at a museum? The Manitoba Children's Museum, in Winnipeg, has a new gallery featuring a high-tech spaceship, a television studio and a graphic-arts studio — all hands-on!

Thursday 30
It's official! Canadian illustrator Barbara Reid has won first prize in the Ezra Jack Keats international competition for the illustration of children's books. She has prize money and a medal to show for it.
☆ **1948** — birth of Murray McLauchlan, pop and country singer

JULY

Extra! Extra!

Forest Offers Glimpses of Long Ago

Scientists are exploring a mummified forest 1100 km from the North Pole, on Axel Heiberg Island, N.W.T. The 45-million-year-old site is special because, unlike other ancient forests in the Arctic, this one hasn't turned to stone. Scientists can easily examine the soft, crumbly wood to determine the forest's history.

Cowboy Poets

About 30 cowboy poets from Western Canada and the United States met recently in Pincher Creek, Alberta, for Canada's first cowboy poetry gathering. The poetry tradition dates back to the Texas cattle drives of the 1870s and shares the stories of ordinary people and everyday things.

Trivia tidbit

Toronto's Collier quints are five months old. Every day they go through 60 disposable diapers and 8 cans of formula (for 30 bottles), and create 2 loads of laundry!

What's *that*?!?   Rockhound

"Rockhound" is another name for a person who's interested in locating and studying rocks, or mineral specimens. Rockhounds also like to study precious and semi-precious stones such as agates and emeralds.

You said it!

"Knock on wood!" Long ago, people believed that spirits lived inside tree trunks. To keep their good luck from suddenly changing to bad, they knocked on a tree and asked the spirits for protection. When you say "Knock on wood!" (or, "Touch wood!"), you mean you don't want your good luck to disappear.

Friday 1

Canada Day
Quebeckers celebrate the nation's birthday with a torchlight flotilla on the St. Lawrence River near Quebec City.
☆ 1952 — birth of Dan Aykroyd, actor

Saturday 2

In Northamptonshire, England, a Japanese car sets a world record for fuel economy by travelling an incredible 2278 km per litre of gas.
☆ 1821 — birth of Sir Charles Tupper, sixth prime minister of Canada

Sunday 3

Loretta the lobster arrives in Nova Scotia. The 150-year-old crustacean was shipped to a market in British Columbia, but her "owner" there decided she'd be happier back in the Atlantic.
☆ 1870 — birth of Richard Bennett, 11th prime minister of Canada

July

Monday 4
Canada Post issues colourful butterfly stamps to mark the 18th Entomology (the study of insects) Congress, in Vancouver, B.C.
☆ 1887 — birth of Tom Longboat, long-distance runner

Tuesday 5
Princess Margaret begins her seventh official visit to Canada with three days in the Maritimes.
☆ 1943 — birth of Robbie Robertson, singer-songwriter

Wednesday 6
Archaeologists digging under the Quebec Basilica have found what may be the grave of Samuel de Champlain, the founder of Quebec City.
☆ 1948 — birth of Lydia Bailey, author of *Mei Ming and the Dragon's Daughter*

Thursday 7
Pictures from space show a massive rock on the planet Mars that is shaped like a human face. Scientists say it may have been carved by a lost civilization.

Friday 8
The Calgary Stampede, the annual 10-day celebration of the cowboy and his world, opens with a parade.

Saturday 9
The top summer movies are *Die Hard*, starring Bruce Willis, and *Short Circuit 2*.

Sunday 10
At the Woodbine Racetrack in Ontario, Julie Krone becomes the first female jockey to ride in the Queen's Plate.
☆ 1914 — birth of Joe Shuster, cartoonist and creator of "Superman"

Monday 11
Emma Houlston, 9, of Medicine Hat, Alberta, takes off from Victoria (with her dad) to try to become the youngest person to pilot a plane across Canada.
☆ 1950 — birth of Liona Boyd, classical guitarist

Tuesday 12
Young Canadian actor Cree Summer Francks heads to California to play a new character, Jennifer, on T.V.'s "A Different World."
☆ 1855 — birth of Ned Hanlan, world rowing champion

Wednesday 13
Ten Ontario residents win trips to Hollywood and the chance to become big winners on the game show "Wheel of Fortune."
☆ 1934 — birth of Peter Gzowski, radio host

Thursday 14
In Tsawwaasen, B.C., golf course workers uncover baskets and other items that may be some of the most important ancient Native artifacts in North America.
☆ 1912 — birth of Northrop Frye, literary critic and professor

Friday 15
Cowboy star Roy Rogers says he's happily retired after 57 years in show biz.
☆ 1902 — birth of Donald Creighton, historian

Saturday 16
Wedding bells ring in Edmonton, as Wayne Gretzky marries actor Janet Jones. And in Vermont, Michael J. Fox ties the knot with actor Tracy Pollan.
☆ 1872 — birth of Roald Amundsen, Arctic explorer

Sunday 17
Four Native bands at Hobbema, Alberta, can now attend their own private institution: Maskwachees Cultural College.
☆ 1935 — birth of Donald Sutherland, actor

July

Monday 18
For the first time in two years, the National Ballet of Canada returns to the Metropolitan Opera House in New York City.
☆ **1911** — birth of Hume Cronyn, actor

Tuesday 19
After nearly two days of swimming, Vicki Keith becomes the first person to swim across Lake Huron. She celebrates with a roast beef sandwich.
☆ **1950** — birth of Jocelyn Lovell, champion cyclist

Wednesday 20
Edmontonians dress in turn-of-the-century costumes for the opening of Klondike Days.
☆ **1951** — birth of Paulette Bourgeois, author of the *Franklin* books

Thursday 21
Trendy sunglasses with hand-painted 3-D characters such as sunbathers, cowboys, and windsurfers on the frames can be yours for only $50 a pair.
☆ **1926** — birth of Norman Jewison, film director

Friday 22
The 11th annual Rockhound Fair opens in Wilberforce, Ontario. Displays of minerals and precious stones from around the world draw crowds.
☆ **1946** — birth of Heather Collins, illustrator of *The Kids Cottage Book*

Saturday 23
Twenty balloonists from Ontario, British Columbia, Quebec and New York take to the skies for the Hot Air Balloon Festival in Newmarket, Ontario.
☆ **1950** — birth of Ian Thomas, singer-songwriter

Sunday 24
As Emma Houlston, 9, touches down in St. John's, Newfoundland, she becomes the youngest person to pilot a plane across Canada.
☆ **1899** — birth of Dan George, also known as Teswahno, actor

Monday 25
Form-fitting Spandex exercise wear has moved out of the gym and onto the street. Fashionable looks include "pop" tops and bike pants.
☆ **1957** — birth of Steve Podborski, alpine skier

Tuesday 26
Fresh from their success in California and New York City, Quebec's Cirque du Soleil entertains Toronto audiences under the big top.

Wednesday 27
In an international survey of geographical knowledge, Canadians rank fifth out of nine nations in locating features on unmarked maps.

Thursday 28
Despite hallucinations about a pool full of marshmallows, swimmer Vicki Keith finishes a 53-hour crossing of Lake Michigan.
☆ **1958** — birth of Terry Fox, Marathon of Hope runner

Friday 29
Twenty-five "mas" (masquerade) bands make final preparations for the Caribana Carnival Parade in Toronto.

Saturday 30
In England, 16-year-old Travers McCullough becomes the first person to solve "Rubik's Clock," the latest puzzle by architect-inventor Erno Rubik.
☆ **1941** — birth of Paul Anka, singer-songwriter

Sunday 31
Scientists at Polar Bear Pass, N.W.T., a national wildlife area, are studying polar bears, muskoxen and hares from a glassed-in observation tower on the tundra.

Extra! Extra!

Eights, eights and more eights!

People around the world associate the number eight with good fortune. Anyone born on the day 8-8-88 is said to be very lucky. Since the day comes around only once each century, there are plenty of celebrations. This year, tourists visited Eighty-Eight, a town in Kentucky, where they could buy 88-cent hamburgers and have a slice of a special cake that was 8 feet, 8 inches long, 8.8 inches wide and 8.8 inches high.

Special Delivery

The popular children's program OWL-TV received an envelope addressed: "To Owl TV, in toronto, intareo, Box 526216." There's no such box number. The stamp was hand-drawn. There was no return address. But it got there!

Trivia tidbit

Marathon swimmer Vicki Keith has 173 penguins in her collection, and her tiny, purple ceramic penguin is with her all the time for good luck. "They're klutzes on land, but once they hit the water they're quite graceful, sort of like me," says Vicki.

What's *that*?!? Lanolin

Lanolin is a yellowish-white fatty substance found on sheep's wool and used in cosmetics, soaps, ointments ... and by swimmers to retain their body heat and protect their skin during marathon swimming in cold water.

You said it!

"He went for it hook, line and sinker."

Hooks, lines and sinkers are items used to catch a fish. If the fish is very hungry or greedy, it swallows not only the bait on the hook, but the line and sinker, too. Since the early 1800s, the expression has referred to someone who is gullible and believes everything he's told.

AUGUST

Monday
1
Civic Holiday
In the summer of 1938, Canadian Elinor Rowins, 5, and American Robert Kernehan, 6, shook hands across the border at the opening of the Thousand Islands International Bridge over the St. Lawrence River. Today, 50 years later, they meet there again.

Tuesday
2
Canadian actor Howie Mandel will star in the movie *Little Monsters*, about a boy who discovers that imaginary creatures are real.

Wednesday
3
In St. John's, Newfoundland, it's time for the regatta on Quidi Vidi Lake. The race is believed to be the oldest sporting event in North America.
☆ **1951** — birth of Marcel Dionne, hockey player

Thursday
4
Hey, kids! For sale: your own battery-powered all-terrain vehicle. It goes 4 km/h, has brakes and costs a whopping $279.99.
☆ **1921** — birth of Maurice "Rocket" Richard, hockey player

Friday
5
In a bid to set a world record, Mike McCarthy of Great Britain parachute-jumps down the short side (54 m) of the Leaning Tower of Pisa, Italy.
☆ **1961** — birth of Linda Hendry, illustrator of *Make It with Boxes*

Saturday
6
Hiroshima Day
Steve Bauer of Ontario wins Le Grand Prix Cyclist des Amériques road race through the streets of Montreal.

Sunday
7
It's macho madness at Maple Leaf Gardens in Toronto as wrestler Randy "Macho Man" Savage defeats Ted "The Million Dollar Man" DiBiase for the WWF heavyweight championship belt.
☆ **1846** — birth of Anna Swan, Nova Scotian giant

Monday
8
In England, the Duchess of York gives birth to a daughter, Beatrice, born at 18 minutes past 8 P.M. on this the eighth day of the eighth month of 1988.
☆ **1947** — birth of Ken Dryden, hockey player

Tuesday
9
A tearful Wayne Gretzky announces that he's leaving the Edmonton Oilers and will play hockey for the Los Angeles Kings.
☆ **1845** — birth of Brother André, Quebec religious counsellor

Wednesday
10
Toronto City Hall hosts a bon voyage lunch for the cast and crew of *The Rez Sisters*, the first Native play (and Native actors) to be invited to perform at the Edinburgh Festival in Scotland

AUGUST

Thursday
11
Bed-and-breakfast? No, bale-and-breakfast! At many ranches in Alberta, riders and their horses can both enjoy hospitality overnight and a full plate (or bucket) in the morning.

Friday
12
In Winnipeg, firefighters have found a new way to clean up spills of hazardous materials — just sprinkle with more than 100 kg of kitty litter and sweep!
☆ **1935** — birth of Brian Doyle, author of *Up to Low*

Saturday
13
For the first time, Toronto's Pakistani community celebrates its homeland's independence day.

Sunday
14
Halifax celebrates its 239th birthday with a four-day bash that includes Canada's largest tea party and Nova Scotia's largest beach party.
☆ **1931** — birth of Brenda Bellingham, author of *Storm Child*

Monday
15
Slathered in lanolin, Vicki Keith crosses Lake Superior in 17 hours. Only Lake Ontario remains on Vicki's list of Great Lakes to conquer.
☆ **1925** — birth of Oscar Peterson, jazz pianist

Tuesday
16
Regina-born blues guitarist Colin James makes his New York debut at Radio City Music Hall.

Wednesday
17
Toronto sailor Jeff MacInnis becomes the first person to navigate the Northwest Passage powered only by the wind and his own strength.
☆ **1964** — birth of Colin James, singer-songwriter

Thursday
18
Back-to-school clothes? Kids are wearing track suits, kilts, lots of black and white, and plenty of western-styled, "Arctic wash" denim.

Friday
19
The team of Dale Evans and Roy Rogers is honoured in Los Angeles by the Western Hall of Fame for 50 years of "corralling big-screen bad guys."

Saturday
20
Popular new consumer products include Personal Facsimile machines for $1799.99 and laptop computers for $1399.99.
☆ **1957** — birth of Cindy Nicholas, marathon swimmer

Sunday
21
In Winnipeg, cyclist Beth Tabor of Calgary wins the women's 1000 m sprint in the National Track championships.

Monday
22
Skater and Olympic silver medalist Brian Orser announces he's turning professional. His new ice show contract makes him the highest-paid Canadian figure skater in history.
☆ **1943** — birth of Vlasta van Kampen, illustrator of *King of Cats*

AUGUST

Tuesday 23
At the Temple of Hera in Greece, the sun's rays light the flame that will travel to the Summer Olympics in Seoul, Korea.

Wednesday 24
A replica of an ancient Greek war ship carries the Olympic flame to Athens on the first leg of the fire's journey to Seoul.
☆ 1920 — birth of Alex Colville, painter

Thursday 25
Nearly seven million corn plants and many hectares of oats have been carved into the outline of Mickey Mouse's head in the fields of Sheffield, Iowa. "Kernel Mickey" is the town's birthday gift to the 60-year-old character.
☆ 1869 — birth of C.W. Jefferys, painter and illustrator

Friday 26
Canada Post's new Dogs of Canada stamps feature four breeds native to this country. The stamps commemorate the centennial of the Canadian Kennel Club.
☆ 1957 — birth of Rick Hansen, wheelchair athlete

Saturday 27
More than 100 Canadians march arm-in-arm with thousands more people in Washington, D.C., to celebrate the 25th anniversary of Martin Luther King's famous march and "I have a dream" speech.

Sunday 28
The McCall-Howard family docks at Harbourfront in Toronto, to end its five-year, round-the-world voyage aboard the boat *Lorca*.
☆ 1913 — birth of Robertson Davies, author

Monday 29
Judas Ullulaq, an Inuit sculptor in the village of Gjoa Haven, north of the Arctic Circle, says he used to use a bone and a stick as his tools, but now he uses electric drills and grinders.

Tuesday 30
Vicki Keith conquers Lake Ontario, becoming the first swimmer to cross all five of North America's Great Lakes.

Wednesday 31
Vicki Keith celebrates her Great Lakes' crossings AND two new swim records: the women's world record of 129 hours and 45 minutes of continuous swimming, and the world record (38 km) for the butterfly stroke.
☆ 1931 — birth of Jean Beliveau, hockey player

SEPTEMBER

Extra! Extra!

Summer Olympics Open

Seoul, the capital of the Republic of Korea (also called South Korea), is the site of the 24th Summer Olympic Games. The spectators and more than 10 000 athletes will be protected by 120 000 specially trained anti-terrorist soldiers, more security than any previous Olympic Games have ever had.

Best-selling Albums in Canada 1988

♪ *Kick*, INXS
♪ *Faith*, George Michael
♪ *Dirty Dancing*, various artists
♪ *Diesel & Dust*, Midnight Oil
♪ *Hysteria*, Def Leppard

Trivia tidbit

Construction workers who have nearly finished building Toronto's SkyDome bring their families to a picnic at the work site. On the menu? 3500 hot dogs, 3500 bags of potato chips and "a truckload of cookies."

What's *that*?!?   Yogurt

When milk is curdled by special bacteria, the result is yogurt, a dairy product that's thick, like pudding. The word "yogurt" is Turkish. People around the world have been enjoying this treat for hundreds of years.

You said it!

"He's playing possum."

When an opossum is chased by predators, it saves itself by pretending to be dead. The opossum seems to be in a trance and can stay that way for several hours. The expression refers to someone who is pretending to be ill or dead, or someone who is pretending not to understand.

Thursday **1**	"The Kids' Radio Club" broadcasts on CKWR-FM, Kitchener, Ontario. The one-hour, weekly program features two kids who play music, read poems and discuss sports, all for other kids. ☆ **1922** — birth of Yvonne DeCarlo, actor
Friday **2**	Vancouver's wedding-of-the-week: Art Williams and Lorraine Jordan say "I do" while standing in a basket on a climbing pole 24 m above the Pacific National Exhibition. ☆ **1965** — birth of Lennox Lewis, Olympic boxer
Saturday **3**	Only 14 more days until the Summer Olympic Games open in Seoul, South Korea. ☆ **1810** — birth of Paul Kane, artist

September

Sunday
4
On Canada Day, Jesse MacLeod of Victoria, B.C., released a red balloon marked with his name and address. He's now received a letter from the Dibb family of Mount LeMoray, B.C., more than 1000 km away!

Monday
5
Labour Day
It's a family affair! Nancy and Karen Kerr win the mother-daughter portion of the Remington Family Tennis Championships in Toronto. Gerard and Yann Lefebvre win the father-son title.
☆ **1916** — birth of Frank Shuster, comedian and partner in Wayne and Shuster

Tuesday
6
Tired of peanut butter? Trendy school lunches are featuring chili, chocolate chip muffins, bagels and yogurt.

Wednesday
7
Tony Esposito, Guy Lafleur, Buddy O'Connor and Brad Park are inducted into the Hockey Hall of Fame.

Thursday
8
Call her Dr. Kain, please. Ballerina Karen Kain receives an honorary doctorate from the University of British Columbia.

Friday
9
Ping-pong is currently the world's second-most popular sport (after soccer). Sixty million people play the game competitively in China alone.

Saturday
10
Albertan k.d. lang wins three prizes at the Canadian Country Music Awards, including her second consecutive prize as entertainer of the year.

Sunday
11
Wild fires and firestorms rage on in Wyoming's Yellowstone National Park. In the past three months the fires have destroyed one-third of the park.
☆ **1944** — birth of Barbara Bondar, author of *On the Shuttle*

Monday
12
Rosh Hashanah
Hannah, Jenny, Kate, Ruth, Lucy and Sarah Walton, the world's only surviving female sextuplets, head off for their first day of school in Liverpool, England.
☆ **1943** — birth of Michael Ondaatje, author

Tuesday
13
Bernie Howgate of Etobicoke, Ontario, is finally home after an 8-year, 23-country tour of the world — on his 10-speed bike.
☆ **1775** — birth of Laura Secord, heroine of the War of 1812

Wednesday
14
A research scientist in Alberta has invented "carrot leather," a new snack food, similar to fruit leathers but made from ... guess what!
☆ **1940** — birth of Barbara Greenwood, author of *A Pioneer Story*

Thursday
15
Athletes from 161 nations take part in the grand march as the 24th Summer Olympic Games open in Seoul, South Korea. Synchronized swimmer Carolyn Waldo carries the flag for Canada.

Friday
16
International Day of Peace
Ed Grimley, a character created by Canadian comedian Martin Short, stars in a new animated cartoon series, "The Completely Mental Misadventures of Ed Grimley."

September

Saturday 17
The Canadian Football League inducts Ralph Sazio, Ed McQuarters, Royal Copeland and Tony Pajaczkowski into the Football Hall of Fame.

Sunday 18
Walkers, joggers, cyclists and others at 2000 sites in Canada and overseas take part in the 8th annual Terry Fox Run to raise money for cancer research.
☆ 1895 — birth of John Diefenbaker, 13th prime minister of Canada

Monday 19
Hear ye! Hear ye! Perry Wamback of Shelburne, N.S., has won the "Best Cry Award" at the International Town Crier Championships.
☆ 1940 — birth of Sylvia Tyson, singer-songwriter

Tuesday 20
Telephone service is now available on North American flights, and authorities say you'll soon be able to phone home from above the ocean!
☆ 1951 — birth of Guy Lafleur, hockey player

Wednesday 21
Yom Kippur
Purple is "in" for fall fashion. Everything from pyjamas to evening gowns comes in shades such as maroon, aubergine, wine, raisin, plum and heather.
☆ 1934 — birth of Leonard Cohen, novelist and poet

Thursday 22
In Ottawa, Prime Minister Brian Mulroney issues a formal apology from the government to Japanese Canadians for the poor treatment they received during World War II.

Friday 23
Ben Johnson wins Olympic gold in the 100 m sprint, and sets a new world and Olympic record of 9.79 seconds.

Saturday 24
The Canadian women's swim team wins a bronze medal in the 4 x 100 m medley relay.

Sunday 25
More medals for Canada! The Canadian men's swim team wins silver in the 4 x 100 m medley relay, and the four-woman dressage team rides to a bronze.
☆ 1932 — birth of Glenn Gould, pianist

Monday 26
The world's wealthiest entertainers? Michael Jackson ($97 million), Bill Cosby ($92 million), Sly Stallone and Eddie Murphy (more than $60 million each).

Tuesday 27
Ben Johnson leaves Seoul, stripped of his gold medal and banned for life from Canada's national team because of illegal steroid use.
☆ 1948 — birth of Mark Thurman, author of *One Two Many*

Wednesday 28
In the White House Rose Garden, United States president Ronald Reagan signs U.S. legislation for the free-trade agreement with Canada.
☆ 1928 — birth of Jean Vanier, spiritual leader

Thursday 29
Carolyn Waldo wins Olympic gold in single synchronized swimming.
☆ 1810 — birth of Sir Hugh Allan, railway promoter

Friday 30
More medals! Carolyn Waldo and partner Michelle Cameron take gold in duet synchronized swimming, and Egerton Marcus wins silver in middle-weight boxing.
☆ 1954 — birth of Sylvia McNicoll, author of *Project Disaster*

Extra! Extra!

Many Twists on Pretzels

A visit to the Bread Museum in Ulm, Germany, reveals all you ever wanted to know about the pretzel. In Germany, pretzels are made in at least 24 different shapes, such as the figure *8* or the letter *B*. Some people say the dough of a standard pretzel is twisted to look like arms folded in prayer. You can eat pretzels dipped in garlic, covered with cheese, and even chocolate-coated!

Top Toys

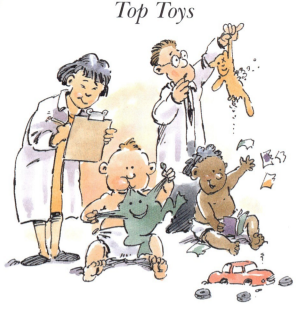

The Canadian Toy Testing Council recommends new toys each year, and 1988's list includes: Ribbitt, a plush frog with a low voice; rubbery Boglin hand puppets; Smooshees, pint-sized friends; and metal mini cars called Color Racers.

Trivia tidbit

In October 1988, 4200 world athletes with a disability gathered in Seoul, Korea, for the 10-day Paralympics.

What's *that* ?!?   Cranberries

Cranberries are tart, red berries that grow in some parts of North America. The fruit got the name "crane-berry" because its stamens look like a crane's beak. Some people turn the berries into sauce, while others add them to muffins or string them for decorations.

You said it!

"Let your hair down!" Many years ago, women never left the house without their long hair firmly pinned up. Only in the privacy of her home (sometimes only in her bedroom) could a woman unpin her hair and truly be comfortable. The expression means to relax, but it also means to be yourself and to speak informally.

OCTOBER

Saturday 1
Mikhail Gorbachev becomes president of the Union of Soviet Socialist Republics.

Sunday 2
At the closing ceremonies of the Olympic Games, Lennox Lewis, winner of Canada's first gold medal in boxing in 56 years, carries the flag. Canadian athletes won three gold, two silver and five bronze medals.

Monday 3
U.N. peacekeeping forces around the world, including 1400 Canadian troops, are awarded the 1988 Nobel Peace Prize.
☆ **1927** — birth of Ashevak Kenojuak, Inuk artist

Tuesday 4
Canadian Liona Boyd is voted best classical guitarist for the fourth straight year in an international poll for *Guitar Player* magazine.
☆ **1934** — birth of Rudy Wiebe, author

Wednesday 5
Thanksgiving grocery shopping: turkey, $3.06 a kilogram; stuffing, $1.09 a box; cranberries, $0.99 a bag; and pumpkin pie, $1.99 each.
☆ **1965** — birth of Mario Lemieux and Patrick Roy, hockey players

Thursday 6
Wayne Gretzky plays his first game (and scores his first goal) with the Los Angeles Kings as they beat the Detroit Red Wings 8–2.
☆ **1769** — birth of Sir Isaac Brock, hero of the War of 1812

Friday 7
The Soviet Union grants official status to the flags and languages of Lithuania and Latvia.
☆ **1930** — birth of Jim Heneghan, author of *Blue*

Saturday 8
There's a new palm-size compact-disc player available. It can play 8-cm discs for two hours.

Sunday 9
The assembly-line concept is 75 years old and still going strong. In 1913 the Ford Motor Company in Detroit started the first line and revolutionized the 20th century.

Monday 10
Thanksgiving
Keith Chapel of Nova Scotia wins the Pumpkin Championship of the World in San Francisco, California. His huge entry sets a new record of 287.4 kg.
☆ **1966** — birth of Karen Percy, Olympic skier

OCTOBER

Tuesday 11
The Winnipeg Humane Society says that rats could become the pet of the future. They're lovable and funny, and don't have to be kept in a cage.
☆ **1929** — birth of Raymond Moriyama, architect

Wednesday 12
Marathon cyclist Joe Tutt of Milton, Ontario, has completed a 6000 km trip to Radisson, Saskatchewan, and back to raise money for the drought-stricken town.
☆ **1934** — birth of Joan Clark, author of *The Moons of Madeleine*

Thursday 13
Ballerina Veronica Tennant announces her retirement after 25 years as a star dancer with the National Ballet of Canada.
☆ **1955** — birth of Jane Siberry, singer-songwriter

Friday 14
Finally, biodegradable garbage bags! The bags, invented in the United States, are strong, but break down in sunlight over time.
☆ **1916** — birth of Andrew Mynarski, World War II hero who earned a Victoria Cross for his bravery

Saturday 15
Entertainers Sharon, Lois and Bram celebrate their 10th anniversary at Nathan Phillips Square, Toronto, with a party hosted by UNICEF. They blow out candles on a 4500 kg cake!
☆ **1701** — birth of Marie-Marguerite d'Youville, founder of the Sisters of Charity of the Hôpital Général in Montreal

Sunday 16
"Mikki Maus" makes his Moscow debut as *Fantasia* is shown there for the first time. Mickey himself (a costumed West German actor) puts in an appearance.

Monday 17
In just two days, Canadian athletes have collected 35 medals at the Paralympic Games in Seoul for competitors with disabilities.
☆ **1948** — birth of Margot Kidder, actor

Tuesday 18
Apples aren't the only fruit growing in B.C.'s Okanagan Valley. Fruit farmer Joe Fernandes has a banana tree in his greenhouse that's over 6 m tall.
☆ **1919** — birth of Pierre Elliott Trudeau, 15th prime minister of Canada

Wednesday 19
Sports "builders" Alan Eagleson and Don Loney, along with hockey star Bobby Hull, pro golfer Sandra Post and figure skaters Barbara Underhill and Paul Martini become members of Canada's Sports Hall of Fame.

Thursday 20
The Los Angeles Dodgers beat the Oakland Athletics four games to one to win the World Series.
☆ **1945** — birth of Jo Ellen Bogart, author of *Daniel's Dog*

OCTOBER

Friday 21

For Sale: the song "Happy Birthday to You." Price: about $14 million. The song was composed in 1893 and earns about $1 million a year in fees.

Saturday 22

Stores can't keep Gucci watches in stock. The $375 item features 12 interchangeable coloured rings for the watch face and a gold-tone bracelet.
☆ 1844 — birth of Louis Riel, Métis leader and founder of Manitoba

Sunday 23

Dawn Nokleby, an Edmonton teacher, loves teddy bears ... and has a collection of 700 bears to prove it! Each one has a name and a special place to sit in Dawn's home or car.
☆ 1963 — birth of Gordon Korman, author of *The Twinkie Squad*

Monday 24

Party leaders Ed Broadbent, John Turner and Brian Mulroney appear in a televised French debate to present their views for the federal election in November.

Tuesday 25

For a second night, candidates Broadbent, Turner and Mulroney debate the issues, but this time the discussion is in English.

Wednesday 26

The United Nations elects Canada to the U.N. Security Council. This step means Canada will play a greater role in world decision-making.

Thursday 27

The most popular movie of all time, *E.T., The Extra-Terrestrial*, is released on video.
☆ 1946 — birth of Ivan Reitman, film director

Friday 28

Rescuers from around the world are still trying to free Crossbeak and Bonnet, two whales that have been trapped in Arctic ice for nearly three weeks.

Saturday 29

Halifax whoops it up at the city's Hallowe'en Mardi Gras. Forty thousand Haligonians parade downtown in costumes and dance in the streets. In all of North America, only New York City has a larger celebration.
☆ 1953 — birth of Denis Potvin, hockey player

Sunday 30

They're climbing the walls at the Calgary Climber's Festival. An indoor, four-storey-high wall at the University of Calgary gives climbers finger jams, bulges and overhangs to clamber over.
☆ 1930 — birth of Timothy Findley, author

Monday 31

Hallowe'en
Trick-or-treaters collect candy and coins for the International Children's Emergency Fund, formerly known as UNICEF. Officials hope to raise $3 million this year to help children around the world.
☆ 1950 — birth of John Candy, actor

Extra! Extra!

What's in a Name?

There's a village in Wales that is famous because of its long name: *Llanfairpwllgwyngyllgogerychwyrndrobwllllantysiliogogogoch*. It means "St. Mary's Church in the hollow of the white hazel near to the rapid whirlpool of St. Tysillios' Church by the red cave." The name has finally been shortened by 38 letters and will appear on maps, documents and signs from now on as *Llanfair Pwllgwyngyll*.

Now Appearing ... Once Every 10 Years!

In Oberammergau, West Germany, reservations are being taken for a play that won't be performed until 1990. For more than 350 years, the citizens of the village have played all 1700 parts in a drama about the passion of Christ that is performed at the beginning of each decade. The citizens also contribute the necessary horses, sheep, costumes and scenery. More than 5000 people see each of the 93 performances.

Trivia tidbit

The longest pool in the world, in San Juan, Puerto Rico, is nearly as long as Toronto's CN Tower is high. It takes almost half an hour to swim its entire curvy length.

What's *that*?!? Richter Scale

This scale was created by Charles Richter in 1935. It uses an earthquake's ground motion (recorded on a machine called a seismograph) to judge the energy released by the earthquake. Moderate earthquakes measure 5; the higher the number, the more powerful the quake.

You said it!

"He was born with a silver spoon."
In the past, the godparents chosen to protect a royal child often gave valuable silver items, such as spoons, as christening gifts. The custom of giving an expensive gift continues in many families, but the expression still refers to someone born <ins>into</ins> a wealthy family.

November

Tuesday 1

A new stamp honours Charles Inglis, Canada's first Anglican bishop, who founded what later became the University of King's College in Halifax.
☆ **1949** — birth of David Foster, singer-songwriter

Wednesday 2

Wake up! Wake up! Toronto's Blue Box recycling program kicks off, and home-owners have to get the boxes to the curb before 7 A.M.
☆ **1960** — birth of Paul Martini, figure skating partner of Barbara Underhill

Thursday 3

Olympic synchronized swimmer Carolyn Waldo has retired from competition and is making commercials for her new collection of activewear.
☆ **1922** — birth of Bernice Thurman Hunter, author of *The Firefighter*

Friday 4

Six-year-old Toronto actor Asia Vieira plays Molly in a new movie, *The Good Mother*. Diane Keaton appears as her movie-mom.

Saturday 5

Wayne Gretzky, newscaster Peter Jennings and game-show host Monty Hall are Canadians on the list of the 10 Best-dressed Men in America.
☆ **1959** — birth of Bryan Adams, singer-songwriter

Sunday 6

Keba is on the list in Toronto's Ward 5 as a registered voter for the federal election. There's just one problem: Keba is a gray schnauzer!
☆ **1867** — birth of Joseph "Klondike Joe" Boyle, adventurer

Monday 7

That Formica on your kitchen counter is 75 years old. Well, maybe not that particular counter, but the product itself was invented in 1913 as an electrical insulator.
☆ **1943** — birth of Joni Mitchell, singer-songwriter

Tuesday 8

It's election day in the United States. George Bush defeats Michael Dukakis to become president with 54 per cent of the popular vote.

Wednesday 9

Quebec announces a plan to eliminate competitive hockey for kids under 12. Growing violence is one of the reasons given.
☆ **1717** — birth of Louis-Joseph Gaultier de La Vérendrye, explorer

Thursday 10

In St. John's, Newfoundland, a week-long expedition to find a giant squid living in Bonavista Bay has failed. The five-man team of scientists will keep looking.
☆ **1845** — birth of Sir John Thompson, fourth prime minister of Canada

November

Friday 11

Remembrance Day

Popular group Blue Rodeo wins five awards at the Toronto Music Awards, including best local and best international group. Bluesman Jeff Healey steals the show with his guitar finale.

Saturday 12

Statistics Canada reports that more than half of all Canadian homes are now equipped with a video cassette recorder and a microwave oven, the two most popular consumer items.
☆ **1606** — birth of Jeanne Mance, founder of the Hôtel-Dieu hospital in Montreal

Sunday 13

The Vancouver Public Aquarium has a new baby whale. The 115-kg, unnamed baby is Canada's first killer whale born in captivity.

Monday 14

There's a new record for the *Guinness World Book of Records*. Over 200 speakers have debated at the University of Toronto for more than two weeks. The topic: "It is worth talking about anything." The debaters beat Oxford University's record of 314 hours of continuous debate set earlier this year.
☆ **1891** — birth of Sir Frederick Banting, co-discoverer of insulin

Tuesday 15

In the spirit of *glasnost* and friendship, Calgarians have raised money to buy a wheelchair for a Ukrainian woman with a disability and have delivered it to her in the Ukraine.
☆ **1969** — birth of Helen Kelesi, tennis player

Wednesday 16

"Sesame Street" starts its 20th year! Luis and Maria are expecting a baby, Big Bird becomes the superhero Blue Bird, and Lily Tomlin will visit the street this season.
☆ **1947** — birth of Ann Blades, illustrator of *The Singing Basket*

Thursday 17

Princess Anne visits the Royal Winter Fair in Toronto. (Mickey Mouse enjoyed a five-day visit to the fair earlier this month!)
☆ **1947** — birth of Petra Burka, figure skater

Friday 18

Former Liberal leader Jean Chrétien is made an honorary chief of the Blood Indian band in Standoff, Alberta. Chrétien is given the Native name meaning "French leader."
☆ **1939** — birth of Margaret Atwood, author

Saturday 19

The holiday movies are coming: Bill Murray's *Scrooged, Cocoon: The Return* and *Ernest Saves Christmas*.
☆ **1937** — birth of Marilyn Bell, marathon swimmer

Sunday 20

Birders meet at Niagara Falls, where gulls like to fish during migration. On a good day, visitors can see nearly 300 000 gulls, including 13 of 19 Canadian species.
☆ **1841** — birth of Sir Wilfrid Laurier, seventh prime minister of Canada

November

Monday 21
It's election day in Canada. Brian Mulroney remains prime minister as the Conservative Party wins 170 of the 295 seats in Parliament.
☆ **1907** — birth of Christie Harris, author of *Cariboo Trail*

Tuesday 22
Special ceremonies in Washington, D.C., mark the 25th anniversary of the assassination of President John F. Kennedy in 1963.
☆ **1950** — birth of Linda Granfield, the author of this book

Wednesday 23
An early-morning earthquake measures 4.9 on the Richter Scale and frightens residents within several kilometres of Quebec City.

Thursday 24
Madam du Cong, a Burmese python and special guest of the Vancouver Opera, attends an opera company luncheon. She will appear in the opera *Aida*.

Friday 25
Flick the switch! In Toronto, Prime Minister Mulroney lights the world's largest Christmas tree (a pole 56 m high). Meanwhile, 40 000 Christmas lights go on at Graceland, Elvis Presley's home in Tennessee.

Saturday 26
Zeke Zzyzus of Montreal has added another *z* to his name. And as Zeke Zzzyzus, he's guaranteed himself last place in the latest Montreal telephone book.
☆ **1938** — birth of Rich Little, impressionist

Sunday 27
In Ottawa, the Winnipeg Blue Bombers defeat the B.C. Lions in a close football game, 22–21, to win the Grey Cup.

Monday 28
How about a new doll for Christmas? Perhaps a Cabbage Patch Toddler Kid, or a Cabbage Patch Doll with "growing hair?"
☆ **1949** — birth of Paul Shaffer, musician

Tuesday 29
At a Toronto gala in her honour, Karen Kain celebrates 20 years of performing with the National Ballet of Canada.
☆ **1818** — birth of George Brown, journalist and politician

Wednesday 30
Believe it or not, teens don't watch more television than anyone else in the family! Statistics Canada says women over 60 spend 35.5 hours a week in front of the T.V. Teens tune in only 19.2 hours during a week. (Kids aged 2 to 11 — 21.4 hours)
☆ **1874** — birth of Lucy Maud Montgomery, author of *Anne of Green Gables*

DECEMBER

Extra! Extra!

Niagara's Festival of Lights

Every December, millions of visitors flock to Niagara Falls, Ontario, to see the world's largest lighting display. The falls themselves are illuminated by 250 million candle-power of coloured lights. The Skylon Tower becomes a huge Christmas tree, with lights on cables that stretch hundreds of metres from the ground to the top. And after a fresh snowfall, every light in this night-time wonderland becomes more magical.

Boxing Day

The celebration of Boxing Day dates back to medieval England, when a box was placed in each church so that people could contribute to charities. The box was opened on Christmas Day and the money inside was given to the local poor by church officials the next day, "Boxing Day." Later, it became the day when wealthy people gave presents of money to servants and anyone else who had performed a service for them during the year. Today, Boxing Day is usually associated with store markdown sales.

Trivia tidbit

The Lego company packed 60 million sets of its popular toy in 1988. Piled on top of one another, they'd be as tall as 10 000 Eiffel Towers, or 400 Mount Everests!

What's *that*?!?   Kissing Ball

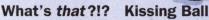

Before Christmas trees became popular in the mid-1800s, people decorated their homes for the holidays with a kissing ball made of evergreens wrapped around wire. Apples, pinecones and dried flowers were added to the ball, which was then attached to the ceiling or a doorway. People kissed under the ball, just the way we smooch under the mistletoe!

You said it!

"Little pitchers have big ears."

There was a time when every household had more than one pitcher, or pouring jug, for daily use. The handle of a pitcher is called an "ear," and often the ear seems very large for the size of the jug. The expression means you should watch what you say when children are listening, and has been in use since the mid-1500s.

DECEMBER

Thursday 1
Canadian actor Leslie Nielsen stars in a new movie, *The Naked Gun*.

Friday 2
Benazir Bhutto is sworn in as prime minister of Pakistan. She is the first woman elected to govern a Muslim nation.

Saturday 3
Black Creek Pioneer Village in Ontario is offering visitors sleigh rides, hot cider and a glimpse of Christmases past.
☆ 1917 — birth of Miriam Waddington, poet

Sunday 4
Chanukah
Mama's Going to Buy You a Mockingbird, written by children's author Jean Little, is now a movie ... and it airs tonight on television.
☆ 1945 — birth of Roberta Bondar, Canada's first woman astronaut

Monday 5
In Vancouver, the 3-week-old baby killer whale dies shortly after being separated from her mother for observation. The calf had been ill for a week.

Tuesday 6
Gary Beacom of Toronto wins the gold medal in the men's final of the world professional figure skating championship in Jaca, Spain.
☆ 1803 — birth of Susanna Moodie, author of the classic *Roughing It in the Bush*

Wednesday 7
Kids in B.C. and the Yukon are writing to Santa Claus and asking for dolls, computer games, video machines, pets and spandex pants.
☆ 1951 — birth of Karen Patkau, author-illustrator of *In the Sea*

Thursday 8
The radio comedy team The Royal Canadian Air Farce celebrates 15 years and 410 half-hour radio shows.

Friday 9
New recordings for gift-giving: *Christmas with the California Raisins*, plus albums by Bananarama, the Bangles, Level 42 and Frozen Ghost.
☆ 1972 — birth of Lori Strong, champion gymnast

Saturday 10
Willie Littlechild, the first treaty Native elected to the House of Commons (for the Alberta riding of Wetaskiwin), plans to speak Cree when he delivers his maiden speech to Parliament.

Sunday 11
The Montreal regional government says it will spend $5000 to change the diet of its police officers. No more fast-food such as greasy chicken and ... doughnuts!
☆ 1964 — birth of Carolyn Waldo, Olympic synchronized swimmer

December

Monday
12

Leslie Nielsen has been honoured with a star on the Hollywood Walk of Fame.
☆ **1938** — birth of Mary Blakeslee, author of *Rodeo Rescue*

Tuesday
13

Blizzard Island is a new Maritime-flavoured kids' adventure series on television. Actual scenes of Nova Scotia forest and sea coast are featured.
☆ **1943** — birth of Ferguson "Fergie" Jenkins, baseball Hall-of-Famer

Wednesday
14

Happy 100th birthday to the Banff Springs Hotel in the Alberta Rockies. In 1888 the hotel had 250 rooms and only 10 bathrooms. Today, there are 834 rooms — and plenty of private bathrooms!

Thursday
15

The last bit of concrete is poured at SkyDome in Toronto, 804 days after the ground was first broken.

Friday
16

Tommy Tricker and the Stamp Traveller, a Canadian film about a kid's treasure hunt, opens in theatres.
☆ **1936** — birth of Karleen Bradford, author of *Windward Island*

Saturday
17

Santa's helpers in Christmas, Florida, are answering more than 20 000 "Dear Santa" letters each day!
☆ **1874** — birth of William Lyon Mackenzie King, 10th prime minister of Canada

Sunday
18

The Supreme Court of Canada has overturned Bill 101, Quebec's language law for French-only signs and ads. Tempers flare across the country.
☆ **1904** — birth of Wilf Carter, singer-songwriter

Monday
19

In Los Angeles, Paulina Mary Jean Gretzky is born, making Wayne a first-time dad.

Tuesday
20

In the news: chickens that are exposed to classical music from birth grow plumper faster than "culturally deprived" birds. So say researchers at Jerusalem's Hebrew University.

Wednesday
21

Winter Solstice
Two Soviet cosmonauts return to Earth after spending a record 366 days in space.

Thursday
22

Patrick Seguin, 16, of Lachute, Quebec, has muscular dystrophy, but that didn't stop him from creating a 40-page comic book called *The Crime Busters*, about intergalactic adventure. It took him nearly three years to complete, it was published, and it's selling out.

December

Friday 23

After years of work, the Canadian Pacific Railway has almost completed the Macdonald Tunnel, a 33.5 km tunnel that passes through mountains and treacherous terrain in British Columbia.

☆ **1930** — birth of Claire Mackay, author of *The Toronto Story*

Saturday 24

"Owen," a wooden statue stolen from a lawn in Oakville, Ontario, has been returned to his owner, but only after travelling to Chicago, New York City and Calgary with his kidnapper. Owen even has photos to prove where he's been.

☆ **1900** — birth of Joey Smallwood, the premier of Newfoundland who led the province into Confederation

Sunday 25

Christmas

The lines are B-U-S-Y! In Ontario alone, 3 million holiday phone calls are made.

☆ **1950** — birth of Isabella Valancy Crawford, author

Monday 26

Boxing Day

"And they're off!" Boxing Day Sales at West Edmonton Mall, the world's largest shopping mall, create a traffic nightmare. Drivers race for one of the 20 000 parking spaces.

Tuesday 27

The Edmonton Oilers win "Team of 1988" by a landslide in the annual sports survey by Canadian Press and Broadcast News.

☆ **1823** — birth of Sir Mackenzie Bowell, fifth prime minister of Canada

Wednesday 28

Don Jamieson of Vancouver collects and restores antique wooden carousel horses. He's got 14 steeds in his home, and he restored a 56-horse carousel for Expo 86.

☆ **1928** — birth of Janet Lunn, author of *The Root Cellar*

Thursday 29

Popular singles in 1988 include: "Don't Worry, Be Happy" by Bobby McFerrin and "Sweet Child of Mine" by Guns N' Roses.

Friday 30

After close to four years of debate, the legislation for free trade with the United States passes the final stage in Canada's Senate and is signed into law.

☆ **1869** — birth of Stephen Leacock, humorist

Saturday 31

It's Gold Rush '88! Rising gold prices bring miners to the Yukon to pan the creeks for gold.

☆ **1947** — birth of Burton Cummings, singer-songwriter